After the Ballet
Jessica Rosevear Fox

Published by
Killing the Angel Press
New Jersey

Cover photo credit: Jessica Rosevear Fox, 2016

Printed in the United States of America.

For our bumblebees

This is what the end looks like.

Two women made their way through Gare de Lyon. The ballerina walked briskly, arrow-straight, pulling an efficient red carry-on behind her. Her hair hung long, combed straight down her back. Her thirtieth birthday had passed a month ago. In her slim purse rested two tickets for a train to take her sister and her from Paris to Avignon.

The ballerina just completed her twelfth and final season with the Manhattan Ballet Company's corps de ballet. She was, in fact, not a ballerina anymore, but she avoided thinking of this.

The second woman trailed behind the first, carrying with her the weight of a failing marriage, of her two children back in New Jersey. She wore a blue felt beret and matching scarf, purchased especially for this trip. Dragging behind, she took comfort in the macaron stands, the racks full of

After the Ballet

Paris Match and postcards covered in glossy Notre Dames and Eiffel Towers. These things made her feel that she could reinvent herself, that a new identity might emerge as the old chipped away. Her large suitcase bulged and thumped along the floor of the crowded train station as she lagged behind her younger sister.

This is how it began.

Two weeks prior, neither Louise nor Helen knew they'd be headed to Saint-Gilles. Learning of Amandine's existence shocked them, much less that she:

    a. was their mother's sister,
    b. owned and operated a lavender farm in France,
    c. that is, until she died recently,
    d. and left the farm to her two American nieces.

Less than a month ago, Helen danced her final performance of *Concerto Barocco* with MBC. Knowing it would be her final of hundreds of performances, she relished the cadence of the steps, the streamlined bodily architecture, the musical yearning. It all seemed desperately alive, even after all these years. The stage's simplicity, the pure white leotards, the sisterhood of the corps, that breathless silence as the curtain rose with all eight ballerinas posed on stage, the authoritative orchestral strings... there came a moment when she wished the music would never end, that she might continue turning and jumping forever. She wished the hamster wheel of more than a decade in the corps would be enough to sustain her. It never would.

She took the extra bow, customary for a final performance, and tried to smile at the energetic applause. Somewhere in the darkened crowd, she knew that her mother, seated alone, clapped for her.

Her only boyfriends, few and far between, had been exclusively within the company. Most recently, Alex, a first generation American with high-profile, Russian dancers-turned-celebrity-ballet-instructors for parents, ended their relationship a month ago, after the announcements for promotions. Alex would be a soloist in the fall; Helen would stay behind in the corps de ballet. He didn't attribute their breakup to the newly disparate caste systems, but within a week, she heard he and Maria Romanovich were together. At twenty years old, Maria had been promoted from soloist to principal, the top level of the ballet world.

"Don't leave over a breakup," her company friends advised. The unsolicited advice insulted

---

her. It wasn't Alex; wasn't it obvious? She'd danced in the corps for twelve years. Twelve years and not a single solo role, always in the background, dancing the same ballets year after year... and now thirty stared her dead in the face. Not only was she old, but she was past the age by which most ballerinas advanced through the ranks, leaving her dying on the vine. Many dancers retired, by choice or by physical necessity, in their thirties, at which point they had to figure out what to do with the rest of their lives. Someone like Maria could be the darling of MBC for decades. Even when she retired, she would probably stay on as a ballet mistress, running workshops and guest teaching. A nobody from the corps didn't stand a chance.

And so she gave her notice to the artistic directors of the company. "This season's *Concerto Barocco* will be my final ballet with MBC," she told them, sitting in the main office, posters of faces not her own covering the walls. "I'm retiring."

They didn't attempt to dissuade her. They smiled, offering congratulations, and presented her with flowers at the last curtain call. As she left that night, she threw them in the dumpster at the back of the theater.

Helen lived with her mother, Matilda, in Nyack,

New York. Her corps salary was nowhere near enough to live in Manhattan unless she wanted roommates, which she did not.

"You don't have to do this," she told her mother the day following her final performance. Louise and her husband were coming over with their two children for a rare family lunch.

"Not celebrate your retirement? Of course we do!"

"It's really not that big of a deal," said Helen. "If it were, Louise would have been there last night."

"Did you ask her to come?"

Helen ignored the question and instead poured a glass from the bottle of wine that sat open and inviting on the counter. "I can't wait to let my body go now."

Louise and Mark arrived, bringing a supermarket cake that read *Congratulations* in pale pink frosting.

"This is for you," Louise offered.

"I hate pink."

As Louise walked into their mother's Victorian on Elysian Avenue, she noticed that Helen seemed a little annoyed. Was it because she hadn't gone to the ballet last night? Louise had given up trying to guess her sister's feelings when Helen couldn't be bothered to communicate anything. What did she want from her? How many times had Louise gone to the city to see Helen dance in *Concerto Barocco*, anyway? Too many to count. She could probably dance the full thing herself. After several years of those performances—along with the usual suspects, *Giselle*, *Sleeping Beauty*, *Serenade*, whatever else— Louise couldn't keep going into the city to watch her sister dancing the same ballets season after season, year after year. She had a life of her own: pregnancies, kids, her house. Waiting for her husband to come home, if he did at all.

"How was the last show?" she tried.

"Fine."

"It was splendid!" Matilda interjected. She rushed toward her grandchildren. "Hello, my darlings!"

Emily, two years old, and Winston, six months, squealed. Louise gratefully handed Winston to her mother and guided a wobbly Emily through the house. "Careful, sweetie," she said, cupping her hand around the sharp edges of the coffee table as Emily toddled through the cozy living room and into the kitchen. Mark sat down on the couch and stared at his phone.

"Maybe now that you're done with ballet, I can expect some grandchildren from you, too, dear," said Matilda, nuzzling Winston, who stared back at his grandmother with wide eyes.

"Speaking of, how is it going with Alex?" asked Louise.

"Awesome," Helen said. "I can't believe you brought a store-bought cake." She couldn't resist a little jab. "You usually out-Martha-Stewart us all."

"So we finally picked a baptism date for Winston," said Louise as she amassed silverware from the buffet drawer.

"When is it?" asked Helen. "I'm very busy these days."

"Really? I thought you'd have a lot of free time now."

"I'm kidding, Louise."

"Right. So I'm planning a little lunch for afterward. You can bring Alex, of course."

"I was joking before. Alex and I broke up."

"Oh," said Louise. "I'm sorry to hear that."

"Thanks."

"Anyway, it'll be you, us, Mom, the Finnegans, and that'll probably be it."

Helen picked up a wad of paper napkins and began setting one down per plate. "I thought the Finnegans were just some random people you knew from church."

Louise hesitated. "Actually, we've chosen Bob

and Carol to be Winston's godparents."

"Oh." Helen paused for a moment before continuing to place the napkins.

"We would have picked you, but..." Louise grasped for words. "It just seemed like you couldn't be that involved..."

"Louise, please. It's fine. I was hardly godparent of the year with Emily."

After being chosen to be Emily's godmother, Helen had missed the baptism because of an injury sustained at a performance the previous night. Father Michael, a strict traditionalist who already opposed the choice of a non-Catholic godparent (Louise and Helen had grown up Unitarians), was not happy and spent his homily lecturing on the importance of commitment not just to God, but to brothers and sisters in Christ. Woe to her who failed her commitments.

Helen apologized as best as she could. After all, how could she stand by the baptismal font when she could barely stand at all? Of course, Louise had said. Don't worry about it. Helen returned to the theater two weeks later, but with time, the resentment hardened in Louise. Never coming with them to church on Christmas Eve because of *Nutcracker* performances, Sunday mornings dedicated to sleeping in following the Saturday evening shows—it wasn't right to make Helen the godmother when ballet was the only god she worshipped.

"Ballet made it hard for me to have any real obligations outside of the theater," Helen continued. "Obviously."

"Yes, and if I had known you'd be retiring, and you had more free time..."

"Just because I'm retired, it doesn't mean I'm going to be sitting around not doing anything."

"I know that. I just—"

Matilda called them for lunch, interrupting the argument they each knew all too well.

Within minutes, though, the phone call that changed everything came. Pierre Bonnot called from his law office in Saint-Gilles, France, delivering the news to Matilda: her two daughters had inherited a lavender farm from a woman named Amandine David.

"I don't understand," said Louise after her mother, visibly shaken, relayed the message. "Who is Amandine?"

"Would you excuse me." Her face grey, Matilda rose from the table and drifted out on to the porch.

"I just want to make sure I have this straight," said Helen. She pressed her fingers against her temples. "That was a lawyer calling Mom from

France."

"Yes."

"The lawyer was calling to tell her that he needed to get in touch with us."

"Yes."

"And he has to get in touch with us because we are now in possession of a farm that was owned by someone named Amandine, and we own it because she passed away and left it to us in her will."

"Yes."

"Was this woman a relative of Mom's?"

"We have the same last name. What else could she be?"

"Then why have we never heard of her?"

Winston began to cry.

"Hon, I think Winston might need to be changed," said Mark, reaching for the rolls.

Louise closed her eyes, then opened them. "Let me deal with this. You go talk to Mom."

"Mom? What are you doing out here?"

Matilda sat on the porch, eyes gazing outward. Ahead, the Hudson River glittered in the twilight. "Just getting my head together." She took a sip of wine from the glass held in her shaking hand.

"Does anything about that phone call make sense to you?"

"It's a ghost."

It was like trying to have a conversation with Emily. "You're not making any sense."

Matilda didn't say anything.

"Unless this is some elaborate scam, Louise and I are going to have to go out to this property." Excitement prickled over Helen's skin. The unanswered questions stung, but the answer *escape* gave way to that long-buried feeling of hope. "It would be helpful to get some information, if you have it."

Matilda said nothing.

"Are we related to this Amandine? She has our last name."

"I haven't seen her, haven't thought about her, in a long time," Matilda murmured. Another sip, another long silence. "She's my sister."

Over the rest of the afternoon, Louise and Helen took turns pressing their mother. How had she never mentioned this sister named Amandine? Were they French? Had she ever been to this farm? Would she come with them when they went there?

Matilda said very little. Their warm, inviting mother vanished with the phone call. When she spoke, she offered riddles. The past is best left in the past. Blood isn't thicker than water. Go to the farm, if you must, but I will not.

14

Saint-Gilles, France.

A wooden scraping woke Helen.

Louise muttered to herself, rummaging through the drawers of the one dresser they shared at the farm's lodge as she mentally sorted through logistics: appraisal, listing, selling, closing. The non-logistics also lingered on her mind. She tried to shove them away.

"Keep it down," Helen mumbled from her pillow.

"How are you still sleeping? It's past eight o'clock."

Helen's body still operated on ballet time, as she called it. Half her nights ended close to midnight, when she fell into bed following a late performance. The next day's warm-up class would start at 11:00, and her commute to the Baryshnikov Theater usually took a half hour from Nyack. "I should be asleep for the next hour and a half. How are you not jet lagged?"

"Aren't you excited to see the farm?"

"We saw it when we got here yesterday."

"We didn't *see* it see it yet."

"Whatever."

Louise had enjoyed a full night of sleep a handful of times since Emily was born two years ago. She woke at all hours of the night, ready to give herself to whoever needed: the baby needed milk or a calming touch, the dog needed to pee, the driveway needed shoveling so Mark could drive to work. "I need to sleep," he'd tell her. There's a very important meeting at work. Clients. Deals. Suits, spreadsheets. "You can sleep during the day, after I leave."

But I can't, she'd silently reply. There is always someone or something that needs me. The phone, the plumber, the dog, the person waiting for a reply text, the baby. Her own mind. Out loud, she'd say, "Okay."

Many times, she thought back to the little job at the tutoring center she worked for a few years following college—managing appointments, matching students and tutors, organizing SAT course schedules, preparing marketing materials. After marrying Mark, she'd quit to dedicate herself to running the household full-time and preparing to become a mother. Her salary wouldn't even cover daycare; what was the point?

But a year passed with no baby, and those listless hours in front of the television, ironing, scrolling through recipes online until her eyes glazed over, began to take a toll. When the second line finally appeared on the stick, she could breathe easily again. For a while.

Now, pulling out a shirt from the wooden drawer as Helen fell back asleep in bed, she wondered if those years were when she started to lose Mark. Maybe those years, before they had kids, were when he lost respect for her. Maybe he never respected her at all. It was hard to tell, and now, looking at her reflection, she pretended it didn't matter, that she didn't care. Unable to keep looking at herself, she turned toward the door.

Coming to Saint-Gilles, she'd been eager to leave something behind, but instead of resting in relief, now the uncertainty of what lay ahead stole her sleep.

"There are three major stages to growing lavender," Laurent explained later that morning. Helen stood at a distance (rudely, thought Louise), sipping coffee from a mug with one hand and shielding her porcelain skin from the sun with the other. "Meaning that it takes three years for the plant to mature. We have a variety of plants at different stages throughout the farm, so I'll show you what each is all about." Laurent worked the farm as Amandine's primary farmhand. At twenty-five years old, he'd been on the farm for seven years, since finishing high school. He'd run farm operations since Amandine's death.

"We don't have to learn how to grow the plants," Helen said. "We're probably just going to sell the farm."

"Even if that's true, we still need to know something about the product we're working with here," said Louise with a frown. The broad, straw hat she'd had the foresight to wear protected her from the Provençal sun.

Laurent took them through the fragrant lines of lavender, rows and rows of purple that intoxicated Louise. How had she gone through life having never visited a place like this? Every second seemed to contain the infinite past, present, and future—so unlike life back home, where each second contained nothing, yet somehow still stretched on gruesomely, eternally.

And now, she owned this piece of heaven. It was hers. For all she stood to lose, this was what she'd gained. As Laurent explained the importance of pruning, the difference between softwood and hardwood, and proper drainage, Louise drifted into her own daydream of what a new life apart from Mark could be. Days spent walking along the lavender plants; leisurely French lunches spent with what were sure to be charming neighbors, their children playing with her soon-to-be bilingual children in the country grass; practicing French with an intellectually advanced tutor who would recommend to her all the books and magazines the cultured literati read.

Not a single smartphone in sight.

"The blossoms look beautiful, but if you do not prune them, if you leave them uncut, the plant will not prosper," Laurent said. He demonstrated, crouching beside a two-year plant. Bees hovered about as he clipped the stems clean with his pruning shears. "Trimming the plant is necessary for encouraging growth in subsequent years. If you keep that up, you'll have a farm of beautiful, healthy plants for twenty, thirty years."

Cutting encourages growth. Cutting is necessary. Helen, refocusing on Laurent, forgot about the brutal sun and stared at the bald shrub. A moment ago, it had boasted a few modest but gorgeous blossoms. Now that Laurent pruned it, it looked tiny and sad. The third year plants one row over, though, looked like that last season, and they now were abundant, vibrant, strong. Cutting got those blossoms here. The strength depended on it.

The moment pushed the thought into her consciousness: *I have no idea what I'm doing.*

Rehearsals, discipline, goals, pointe shoes, performances: these things she knew. She knew the razor-like focus needed to achieve a goal. She did not know what remained once the pointe shoes disappeared, what purpose remained once the goal muddied.

"You could always teach." She must have heard that line a hundred times after news of her retirement got out. Not that she ever solicited advice, but everyone seemed to want to give it anyway. She had no desire to teach. She loved her niece and nephew but found children, in general, needy and irritating.

"Now you can do what you really want," was another unwelcome, oft-repeated line—usually from people outside the ballet world. What she really wanted was to be a principal dancer. Anything she did from here on out would be a mere job, something to make money, never a career. She didn't want a twenty-year career in the corps, and that meant leaving. She fought hating the twenty year olds, the Maria Romanoviches, girls who danced for a few years and rose through the ranks while she turned thirty years old in the corps, receiving their sympathetic looks, their whispers. It didn't seem fair, but the years spent had nothing to do with it. She lacked the technique, the artistry, the musicality, who knows what. The clock's ticking slowed. She pruned her life, and as she switched looking back and forth between the second and third year plants, inspiration flashed.

"What do you know about failure?" asked Louise later that night as they stood in the lodge kitchen, preparing dinner. "You're barely thirty years old. You're just a baby. Try being thirty-four."

"In the ballet world, I'm geriatric," Helen said, stirring dressing into the tossed salad.

"Please," scoffed Louise. "You could have stayed."

"You don't know what it's like. Imagine you're in an entry level job for ten years. And your boss keeps telling you that maybe one day, you'll advance, but you also might never advance. Oh yeah, and you're the age when people start thinking about retirement."

"You knew that going in."

That stung. "Thanks a lot."

"Sorry," said Louise. "It's just funny hearing you talk about this, because I'm pretty sure Mom said this same thing to you about a thousand times before you left for the company."

Louise was right. Helen could remember her mother saying everything that would aggravatingly come true: *you need a backup plan, what happens if you become injured, the span of even the most successful career is so short.* Absolutely nothing

21

would dissuade her; in fact, each warning served as more reinforcement to her resolve. Amazing how the life she just left behind mirrored the exact one she'd dreamed of for so long. After a while, the dreams of a child weren't good enough anymore.

"I shouldn't be one to lecture," Louise said. "I'm thinking of leaving Mark."

Helen froze, thoughts of her years in the corps scattering. "Excuse me?"

"Let's eat." Louise lifted a platter of chicken she'd prepared. "I'm going to need my strength."

The story came out over dinner, eaten on the patio furniture outside under the comforting buzz of cicadas, the lines of lavender stretching into the distance. Louise lit a cigarette.

"Since when do you smoke?" Helen asked, incredulous. First Mark, now this.

"Mark's been making me crazy." Louise ignored the question, inhaling and exhaling.

Watching her, Helen craved a cigarette. She quit five years ago. Looking out at the lavender helped. "Crazy how?"

"You know what I mean."

Nothing came to mind, besides the sheer fact that Mark was boring. She figured he'd always been that way. The truth was that she didn't know

Mark very well. She'd been in the company for a year when they married and only saw him on holidays. Even then, he usually spent most of his time reading the newspaper in a room apart from everyone. Most other times she saw Louise, it was just her, Emily, and now Winston. "I'm not sure I do."

Louise exhaled, then stubbed out her cigarette. "It's too pretty to smoke out here."

"What's the problem with Mark?"

"He's disconnected. Disengaged. It doesn't even feel like a marriage anymore. It's like a hollow tree, and one gust of wind will just blow it down. I'm tired of it."

Helen remained silent. She didn't know what to say.

"He leaves me, you know," Louise added. "Every once in a while. Sometimes it'll just be that he gets home at midnight without any explanation. I ask him and he doesn't answer. But sometimes he's gone for a day, or two days, or three. The worst was four days with barely any communication."

She'd never mentioned that before. Everything always seemed so perfect with Louise, with her nuclear family, a husband that worked nine to five, a suburban home. Their mother liked to nag Helen to be more like Louise, even back in high school when Helen would spend every night in the studio while Louise stayed home doing homework or on the phone with her girlfriends. Louise never had to miss family functions because of rehearsal or performances. But it looked like she, for the first time, was in the same place as Helen: starting over. "Oh, Louise," was all Helen could say.

"This first time he was gone overnight, I filed a missing person's report. I mean, what other explanation could there have been? He hadn't bothered to tell me he'd be gone for two days." She shook her head. "He came back and gave some excuse. But then it happened again a few weeks later. This time he texted every few hours just so I would know enough not to file a police report, but not enough to know where he was or who he was with. He's been pulling this for almost a year."

"A year!" Helen exclaimed. "And you just sit there and take it?"

"You don't understand. I wanted to give him the benefit of the doubt at first. He threw a lot of guilt stuff at me when I would get angry and demand more than just 'I was out.' Didn't he deserve his own life, doesn't he provide for us, a lot of that stuff. As if I was the one causing him pain. Not anymore. I've had it."

"Do you think he's cheating?"

"I have no idea," Louise said. "No idea. But I'm done trying to figure it out."

"Have you filed for divorce yet?"

"No," she said. "But I'm going to when we get back to the States."

"And Emily and Winston?"

"I started keeping documentation of every time Mark left us for days at a time. I've been building a case for a while now that would help me get full custody."

"You're really serious about this, aren't you?"

"I haven't committed to one decision either way. I just want to be prepared for every scenario." She gave Helen a sideways glance. "I don't take this lightly, you know."

The sisters sank in silence.

"What are you really doing here, Louise?" asked Helen finally.

"Settling Amandine's affairs."

"And how long are you planning on staying?"

Louise leveled her eyes with Helen's. "How long are you?"

Neither of them could answer, and they allowed their gaze to drift back over the lines of lavender working their way toward sunset.

Later that night, Helen heard Louise fighting

with Mark on the phone.

"I don't know when I'll be coming back... yes, I understand... well, take the kids yourself. I just..."

She stormed into the living room and dropped onto the sofa next to Helen.

"What'd he say?"

"Emily's starting to ask when I'm coming back."

"What'd you tell him?"

"I said I didn't know yet, that we're still wrapping things up. He said she's missing Sunday school because I'm not there to take her."

"Why doesn't he take her?"

"Mark doesn't really go to church with us."

"I don't understand."

"He goes sometimes, but I mostly bring the kids."

"But you converted for him."

"I didn't do it for him," said Louise, defensive. "I did it for me."

"Sure you did."

"Come on, Helen. Our religious upbringing was a joke."

"It wasn't!"

They'd attended a Unitarian church, or some called it a congregation, and it had none of the elements that Emily and Winston would experience growing up Catholic. There was a lot of zen meditation, a lot of poetry, a lot of political activism. Most of the congregation members hailed from many other various religions: former Muslims, Methodists, Hindus, Jews. Their mother called herself an alumni of Catholicism.

"How can you say we had a strong religious foundation when it's a tradition whose tradition is no tradition? People leave their traditions to become Unitarians."

"I love how you're so bent on tradition, but you're hiding from your husband, whom you plan on divorcing, on a French farm. I'm sure Saint Holier-Than-Thou Church will love that one."

Louise's childhood Sunday school teachers had spent a lot of time emphasizing that "some people believe in God—theists—and other people don't believe in God—athiests—and that's okay." She remembered that speech vividly, as it was delivered many times. However, there wasn't a lot about what God actually was, what God felt like, what experiencing God meant, beyond the intellectual analysis. She welcomed Mark's imperative to convert to Catholicism, and was thrilled that her children would have a clearly defined spiritual path to grow up on.

But Mark got lazy. He didn't want to go to mass, but became irritated if Louise skipped. He didn't want to say the Our Father at bedtime with Louise and the kids—he was tired, he needed a minute, go on without him. As Louise's faith in her husband slipped away, her faith in her religious path had wavered, too. She remained the picture of a dutiful housewife; she attended mass. She cooked the meals; she confessed her sins. She told her children, "Daddy loves you"; she told them, "Take this holy water." She began to wonder if it was a conversion of convenience, yet another example of her bending to circumstances life presented her instead of creating them herself.

Similarly, Helen may have grown up in the Unitarian church, but she'd developed into a new religion of discipline, self-control, one entirely of her own making. Ballet became her religion, no doubt about it, with its own daily prayers, offerings, sacrifices, worship. Choreography was her catechism, muscle pain her forty day fast.

As these constructions fell away, the question *What remains?* lingered.

The cool air, perfumed with the scent of lavender and the soft buzzing of the cicadas, wafted through the bedroom window that night. Asleep, Louise snored and twisted in bed. Helen lay awake, eyes on the ceiling, one hour passing, two hours passing.

At least Louise slept, if not soundly. Helen turned on her side. How much longer did Louise want to stay in France, on this farm? A quick sale would give them a little bit of money, and Helen could use that to start over as she pruned the beautiful blossoms of her own life in order to preserve and thrive. It's not as if ballerinas got pensions. They could enlist Pierre Bonnot, Amandine's lawyer, to coordinate the sale and rake in the profits in no time. The farm had to be worth something.

As she finally drifted asleep, Helen slipped into a dream. She dreamed about Amandine in the likeness of the one photo she managed to find, after much searching, in an obituary online from a local French newspaper. In her dream, she and Amandine danced together through the lavender field to the music of Bach. Her face obscured by wind-whipped hair, Amandine swirled and twirled, staying just out of reach of Helen. She woke up at dawn in a sweat, and felt... what was it? Sadness, longing? Was it possible to miss someone you'd never met?

The following day, Pierre Bonnot, seated at the desk in his office on Rue Jacques d'Uzès, gave

Louise and Helen as much information about aunt Amandine as he could.

Amandine and Mathilde had grown up on the lavender farm as children.

What?

Their parents ran the farm, and when they had died, Amandine took over.

But why did Mom—Mathilde—leave France? She has no accent. She goes by Matilda.

Pierre flipped through his notes as he told them the story.

Amandine said her sister fell in love with an American tourist and returned to the States with him when she was nineteen years old. It devastated the family when she left their country, their farm behind. She started a life for herself apart from everything that meant anything to her family.

Our parents never married. We never knew our father.

Amandine was a wonderful business woman, Pierre said. She sustained the farm during the hard times, maintained solid relationships within different regional industries that used lavender and bought from her farm. About ten years ago, she began hosting events on the property, especially weddings. Within six months, the farm was hosting weddings every weekend in the summer, when the lavender was in full bloom. Just gorgeous. She was featured in several French bridal magazines. She was sixty-five when she died.

What'd she die of?

Her heart, said Pierre. It weakened over time. Her ashes are scattered under the oak tree in the southernmost farm fields.

Louise remembered that tree from the tour with Laurent—firmly planted, ancient, maybe even wise, reaching for the sky. It seemed a tree that would share the secrets of the universe if one sat underneath its branches long enough, like the stories of the Buddha she'd heard in Sunday school as a kid.

Did our mother know about the funeral?

No. They hadn't been in touch for years, but Amandine spoke of her sister and her sister's family often. Before she had children, before their parents died, Mathilde visited the lavender farm every year. Apparently, when Louise and Helen were born, Amandine pressured Mathilde to return to their roots, return to the farm, especially since by then both of their parents had passed away. Mathilde refused, and a wedge formed between them. That may explain why she never spoke of her history in France, Pierre Bonnot said, concluding the story.

Helen felt disappointed. So Amandine had inherited this farm. After her dream the previous night, she'd hoped that it was a sign that a connection was forming. Is it possible to have a relationship with someone who already died, someone who you never had a chance to meet? Perhaps part of her longed for it. But the mystery was gone now—Amandine inherited the farm, just as Helen inherited it. What good is inheritance? Something you don't work for at all, something that falls into your lap. She thought back to the twelve years she spent working her body to the bone every day, and how it felt like it amounted to absolutely nothing. "I need to get out of here," she muttered to Louise.

But Louise looked entranced. The thread of truth this story offered stitched together the scattered, fraying pieces of her life. She heard her own voice saying, "We're found."

"How can you feel like that went well?" Helen asked as she drove them along the country road back to the farm.

"Don't you see? We're part of something bigger than we ever thought. We're part of a legacy." Reflecting on the past decade of her life, Louise saw that she had been living passively, a lump of clay molded according to whatever artist's hands happen to attain her. She had wanted to blame others: growing up, Helen's artistic temperament took center stage in their family; Mark's desires, even his whims, overpowered her will in their home; her job hadn't paid enough to stay, so she'd felt forced to quit. Feeling like a powerless victim of circumstances, she'd bent to the myriad winds that came and went in her life without knowing she was part of something so much larger: a mother so passionate she'd leave behind everything she knew, an aunt whose love for her nieces meant they remained in her history, in her legacy, no matter how much time and space existed between them. "We have a transcendent connection," Louise said, vocalizing her thoughts.

Helen gave her a sideways glance. "Okay, weirdo."

Louise let out a laugh. They shed their weight somewhere between Paris and Provence, as though the velocity of the bullet train outstripped the resentments and problems that calcified over the years. Though they didn't admit it to one another, the two women began to feel like the kids they'd been back on Elysian Avenue so many years ago, teasing and annoying each other, walking to school together.

"I want you to teach me ballet," Louise said.

"You want to learn ballet? From me?" asked Helen, incredulous.

"Yes." The taste of connection lingered on Louise's tongue; she longed for more. "When we get back to the lodge. You can teach me. I want to learn."

"But why?"

Louise looked out the window as the scenery of their ancestors whipped past. "I feel this force... it's hard to explain. It's something I can't escape, but at the same time, I don't want to escape it. No matter what we do or don't do, there's this thing we're part of that's connecting us to each other. At the same time, though, it lives fully in each of us."

"I think I know what you mean." Helen told her about the dream of Amandine in the field, about feeling for, and, perhaps paradoxically, remembering, a life unknown.

"Yes, exactly," said Louise. "I just think, here we are, across the world, held together despite years of effort against it, by a woman who never really even knew us, and yet, we were part of her simply by virtue of who we are. It's not anything special that we did to deserve it. There were no Christmas cards or birthday phone calls, or anything like that. But something meaningful was there anyway. It's

34

almost like we're part of something, but not by choice. Except I want it to be by choice, too, Helen. I feel the force of the connection in spirit, but I want to feel it for real, between you and me, sisters."

A moment passed before Helen spoke. "I'd like that, too."

And so they stood, sister facing sister in the kitchen, the length of the kitchen table their barre. Helen's phone played classical music.

"First position. Heels together."

Louise adjusted her feet. "Like this?"

Ordinarily, she might have laughed, but a tenderness pierced Helen as she beheld her older sister's stiff frame, attempting the very basics of the art she'd spent her life trying to perfect. "Yes, but fix your turnout." Some things require practice; others require tapping into something that was always there.

"What's turnout?"

"Don't twist your feet. Keep them perfectly straight, and then rotate your whole leg. You should feel everything opening up."

Louise tried again. "Yes. Now I feel it." She heard cracking as her knees dipped into her very first plié and knew she was too old to be doing this.

But she wanted to, and so she would. She pliéd again and felt strong, dipping and rising.

"And second position." Helen watched Louise stretch toward the makeshift barre, and a divide, forged long ago, started to close.

At twilight, she walked along the rows of lavender, out to the oak tree and sat beneath it. The creatures of night sang; the clean aroma of lavender filled the air; the violet blossoms soothed her soul. She thought of Amandine, strong-willed and steady, sitting under this very tree, looking out at the purple lines, seeing her parents in them, just as Helen now saw her grandparents, her aunt, even her mother in the fields. She saw herself; she saw her sister; she saw Emily and Winston. She could sit at the foot of this oak tree, not moving, not planning, not working, and by the mere blessing of existence, feel the profound meaning in not just her own life, but the lives from whence she came, the rich inheritance running through her, from those who had passed, those who lived, and those who had yet to live.

About the Author

In 2011, Jessica Rosevear Fox founded *Killing the Angel* magazine, an annual literary magazine inspired by Virginia Woolf. This is her first publication through Killing the Angel Press, which she founded in 2016. Find her online at www.killingtheangel.com, on Twitter at @killingtheangel, or via email at killingtheangelmagazine@gmail.com.

About the Author

www.ingramcontent.com/pod-product-compliance
Lightning Source LLC
Chambersburg PA
CBHW020610130626
46552CB00007B/3130